Sean

W9-CCM-227

WALT DISNEY'S

THE ARISTOCATS

Based on Walt Disney Company's
full-length animated feature film

This adaptation by
Victoria Crenson

TROLL ASSOCIATES

Chapter One

One mild Spring morning a long time ago, an elegant coach clattered over the cobbles in the best district of Paris. Seated in the carriage was a kindly, handsome lady. Her white hair sparkled like frost beneath a wide-brimmed hat, her beautiful dress was the height of fashion.

Sharing the carriage with Madame, was a gorgeous snowy-white cat and her three beautiful kittens. Duchess, the mother of the three furry bundles of mischief, sat on a velvet seat. Her blue eyes flashed with pleasure as the carriage rolled along the broad avenues of Paris. Marie, the female kitten, was pure white like her mother. She sat in the crook of Madame's arm.

Toulouse and Berlioz, Marie's brothers were, as usual, up to mischief.

Driving the carriage was Edgar the butler. He was a thin man with a wrinkled face. He was smiling grimly as Toulouse, a gold kitten, tried to climb onto his nose, a painful experience. Edgar was patient with the kittens only because he wanted to gain Madame's favor. Berlioz, a ball of smoky-gray fur, was trying to climb out of the carriage onto the horse's back.

Frou-Frou, who was a good-natured

horse, glanced over her shoulder and neighed. She loved Duchess and her family and she enjoyed taking them on an outing on such a lovely day.

Madame petted Marie. "Marie, my little one, you're going to be as beautiful as your mother. Isn't she, Duchess?"

Duchess nodded and lifted her tail like a splendid fan. "Meow," she answered, rubbing against Madame.

"Careful, Toulouse," warned Madame suddenly with a laugh. "You're making it very difficult for Edgar." The gold kitten clung on to the end of the butler's hooked nose. Grabbing him by the scruff of the neck, Edgar threw him on to the carriage floor. Berlioz was now on Frou-Frou's back nibbling a flower on her hat.

The carriage turned into a short, elegant street and up to a tall stone mansion.

Duchess gazed at her kittens. One could never be sure of their behavior. They were so young and still had a lot to learn. It wasn't easy teaching them to live up to the name "Aristocats."

Edgar jumped to the pavement and helped Madame from the carriage.

Duchess waited on the pavement carrying her tail proudly. "Berlioz," called Duchess sweetly. "Haven't you forgotten something, darling?"

Berlioz remembered his manners and looked up at the mare. "Thank you, Miss Frou-Frou for letting me ride on your back."

Frou-Frou gave a deep throated chuckle. "You're quite welcome, young man."

Edgar opened the door leading into the mansion. "Duchess...kittens. Come along!" said Madame.

Obediently, the cats ran into the hall. Inside the mansion was as grand as the outside.

Madame paused at the foot of the curving staircase. "Oh, Edgar, I'm expecting my attorney George Hautecour.You remember him, of course!"

Edgar raised one eyebrow. "Of course, Madame. How could anyone forget him?" Edgar thought the old lawyer was a kook.

Minutes later George Hautecour's flashy yellow and gray car pulled up outside the gates of Madame's mansion. His black top hat, long scarf, bright green coat and scarlet stockings made him look like a wrinkled tropical bird.

Edgar, wearing a sickly smile, answered the door. "Ah, good day, sir. Madame is expecting you."

Walking unsteadily towards the stairs, the lawyer called, "Come on, Edgar. The last one up the stairs is a nincompoop."

"Ah, couldn't we use the elevator this time, sir?" asked Edgar.

The attorney was already on his way up the stairs. "Poppycock! Elevators are for old people. Whoops!" He clutched at the banister, missed his footing and fell backwards.

Gritting his teeth, Edgar rushed forward and caught him. Then the old man jumped on Edgar's back and had the butler carry him up the stairs piggyback. Edgar thought today would be as grim as it always was when Monsieur Hautecour paid a visit.

Chapter Two

Madame was in her boudoir when she heard a sharp knock at the door. Edgar opened the door and stumbled inside. "Announcing Monsieur Hautecour."

"So good to see you, George," said Madame in a sweet voice.

George beamed. "Ah, still the softest hands in all of Paris, eh?" He was unaware that he was clutching Duchess's tail.

"Now George, do sit down. I've asked you to come here on a very important legal matter."

George picked up his briefcase and stumbled over to the ornate desk. "Who do you want to sue?" he asked.

"I don't want to sue anyone. I simply want to make my will."

"Will, eh?" said George picking up his pen. "Now then, who are the beneficiaries?"

Madame sat up straight. "Well as you know, I have no living relatives and, naturally, I want my beloved cats to be always well cared for. Certainly no one can do this better than my faithful servant, Edgar."

Edgar was below stairs in the servant's quarters. On the wall close to him hung the speaking tube Madame used to call him. Now, quite clearly, he heard his name mentioned. He rushed over to the tube, picked it up and listened. Loud and clear he heard the lawyer's voice say, "Adelaide, you mean you're leaving your vast fortune to Edgar? Everything you possess, this mansion, your country house, jewels?" Edgar's eyes lit up like a Christmas tree.

"No, no George." Madame's voice was gentle but firm. "Not to Edgar - to my dear cats! I simply wish to have the cats inherit first. Then, at the end of their lifespans, my entire estate will revert to Edgar."

The butler's shoulders sagged. Dropping the speaking tube, he slumped down on to a trunk mumbling, "Cats inherit first and I come after the cats...it's not fair. Oh...each cat will live about twelve years, I can't wait... and each cat has nine lives. That's four times twelve multiplied nine times. No, no I'll be gone by then."

Then a wicked thought occurred to him and he chuckled. Then he began to laugh out loud in glee. There was one way to make certain that he was the one to inherit. "They'll be gone, I'll think of a way. There's a million reasons why I should," he giggled. His greedy eyes lit up with dollar signs. "Millions," he drooled. "Those cats have got to go." Then he carefully thought out a plan.

Edgar was determined to get rid of Duchess and her kittens as soon as possible. Madame would grieve, but she'd get over it. Then Edgar would inherit her fortune. He chuckled, a cold evil sound, and poured a handful of sleeping tablets into the pan of creamy milk he was

warming on the stove. As he stirred he hummed, "Bye kitties. Bye-bye you go. La,la,la,la, and I'm in the dough. Oh Edgar, you sly fox," he said to himself. He didn't have long to wait now. He poured the brew into the cats' feeding bowls.

Duchess was helping her kittens with their painting and piano lessons when Edgar opened the door and peered in. He carried a tray covered by a cloth. "Ah...good evening my little ones," he cooed in an oily voice.

11

The three kittens bounded onto the floor, rubbing against the butler's ankles. It was dinnertime...their tummies told them so. "Meow! Meow!" they cried.

In a bland voice the butler said, "Here is your favorite dish prepared a very special way - creme de la creme a la Edgar." Placing the dish in front of the kittens, he murmured, "Sleep well, I mean, eat well, of course."

Duchess also meowed her thanks for the meal. They all started sipping from the dish. At that moment a tiny mouse known as Roquefort, peeked out of his hole. He was a very smart mouse and liked Duchess and her family. They were all good friends and he could trust them. He pushed his gray and white body through his doorway, long black whiskers twitching, his nose wrinkling. The smell of Edgar's cooking had attracted him.

Loudly he cleared his throat. "Good evening, Duchess. Hello, kittens."

Marie stopped lapping. "Hello Roquefort," she called. Toulouse, his mouth full also called, "Hi, Roquefort!"

The little mouse sniffed the air. "Something smells very good."

"Oh, Monsieur Roquefort, won't you join us?" invited Duchess.

The mouse pretended to look surprised. "Ah..it so happens I have a cracker with me..thank you, don't mind if I do. Just a few dunks... Mmm!...this calls for another cracker. I'll be right back."

Berlioz yawned. My...he did feel sleepy all of a sudden and it wasn't even bedtime.

Roquefort's mouth opened in a wide yawn. He felt so tired and his front door seemed such a long way off. He yawned again. "Oh dear, whatever is the matter with me?" He finally staggered through his doorway. He thought, "So that's creme de la creme a la Edgar." Then the mouse began to snore.

Chapter Three

It was late at night when Edgar stuck his head around the delivery door at the side of the mansion. Luck was with him - there wasn't a soul in sight. He didn't want anyone to see him. Turning back into the kitchen, he lifted up a basket draped with covers and tiptoed quietly into the night. During the evening he had left his motorcycle and sidecar near the road, and now he placed the basket in the sidecar. He pulled the covers aside to peep in at Duchess and the kittens. They lay in a deep slumber. All had worked according to plan. Edgar quickly dropped the covers back into place, jumped on his motorcycle and started the engine. The sooner he was out of the city, the better.

Soon the city streets were left far behind as Edgar headed for the open countryside. On and on he drove. He wanted to make sure that Duchess and her family would never find their way back to Paris. The greedy butler didn't care what happened to the cats. All he could think of was money... tons and tons of money...and all his!

He drove across a bridge. Just ahead, black against the sky, stood a windmill. He headed straight for it.

Edgar did not know that the windmill was home for two dogs - Lafayette, an extra long dachshund, and Napoleon, a huge bloodhound with a sad droopy face. Napoleon, snoozing under a hay cart, lifted his head. Some unusual sound had disturbed him.

The bloodhound listened carefully then sat straight up, bumping his head on the bottom of the cart. "Lafayette! Hey, Lafayette!" he called softly.

"Uh..." growled the dachshund. "I'm right here."

"Listen! Wheels coming!" He cocked his ear, listening hard. "It's a motorcycle. Two cylinders, chain drive, one squeaky wheel on the front it sounds like." Napoleon was proud of his excellent hearing.

The two dogs moved towards the road. "Now you go for the tires...and I'll go right for the seat of the problem." Napoleon loved biting holes in trousers.

"How come you always grab the tender part for yourself?" grumbled Lafayette.

"Because I outrank you, that's why," replied Napoleon. "Now stop beatin' your gums and let's attack," he grunted. "Ready, charge!" and with a mighty leap he jumped clear over Lafayette and raced up the road. The two dogs, whooping and barking, chased the motorcycle.

Edgar glanced over his shoulder. Dogs? In this lonely spot? They were gaining on him and one was very large. He tried to swing his motorcycle around to go in another direction but he skidded down a steep hill towards the river. The basket containing Duchess and the kittens tipped

and fell with a thud on the ground. Duchess and two kittens, still sleeping, rolled out.

Thoroughly frightened, Edgar rode into the water. Yelping with excitement, the dogs followed. Across the river, up a bank, over the bridge went Edgar, the two dogs chasing him. He hit a bump, flew through the air and landed back on the driver's seat. Shaken, he turned his head and his eyes opened in horror - he had two unwanted passengers... Napoleon and Lafayette were riding in the sidecar.

Edgar yelled and leaped onto the handlebars. Leaning forward, Napoleon took a hefty bite out of the seat of the butler's pants.

"Nice doggy! Nice doggy!" screeched Edgar. But Napoleon could not be bribed. He took another nip. A wild chase followed. Lafayette, trying to nip the butler again, almost got his paws squashed. The dachshund got his own back by chomping on Edgar's leg.

"Ouch! Yeow!" screamed the butler. He roared off into the night as fast as his motorcycle could go. Bitten, shoeless, hatless, his umbrella lost, his pants torn, he knew he must get back to Paris before dawn...before anyone saw him in such a state. Besides he must be at his post in case Madame missed him.

Without warning, the weather suddenly changed. A few heavy drops of rain fell.

Duchess, stretched out limply beside the river opened her eyes. The cold rain helped wake her. Blinking, she shook her head and stood up. From a distance came the first rumblings of thunder and she arched her back in surprise. "Oh...oh, where am I?" she meowed. "I'm not at home at all!" She called anxiously, "Children, where are you? Answer me!" No sound came to her except the drip of rain. Fear clutched at her heart. What had happened to her family? "Berlioz...Toulouse...Marie! Where are you?" she cried.

"Here I am, Mama."

Duchess ran forward. Marie was caught in a tree. "Marie, darling...are you all right?" Duchess climbed the tree to rescue her damp daughter.

Marie shivered. "I guess I had a nightmare and fell out of bed." The frightened kitten snuggled close to her mother.

"Mama!" came another frightened cry.

"That's Berlioz," said Marie. Duchess and Marie searched the bushes.

"Don't worry, darling. Everything's going to be all right." Duchess's voice sounded brave but deep inside she had a feeling of dread. Where were they? How could this terrible thing have happened?

Berlioz came from the water, a miserable-looking kitten. "I'm coming, mama. Gee...I'm cold and wet."

Duchess led her two kittens to the basket lying close to the river. "Now just stay here while I go and look for Toulouse."

There was a movement under the covers draped over the basket and suddenly a small gold head emerged, blinking sleepily. "Toulouse!" Marie cried.

The kitten sat up rubbing his eyes. "I was having a funny dream. Edgar was in it and we were all riding and bouncing along...uh, oh!" he said looking around at the basket and the river. "It wasn't a dream. Edgar did this to us."

"Edgar?" Duchess frowned. "Oh darling, that's ridiculous."

The thunder began to roll again. The cats looked up at the sky and even Duchess felt scared in this strange place. Marie ran under her mother's furry tummy. "Mama, I'm afraid.I want to go home," she squealed.

Duchess knew better than to let her

little family see that she too, was scared. "Now, now my darling, don't be frightened," she whispered.

Suddenly the sky opened up and the rain poured down in sheets. "Oh dear, let's get into the basket, all of us." Quickly she moved the kittens towards shelter. Damp and shivering, Duchess and the kittens huddled beneath the covers.

Toulouse peeked out. "What is going to happen to us?"

Duchess shook her head sadly. "Darlings, I just don't know." She sighed a long, very sad sigh. "Poor Madame. She will be so worried when she finds us gone."

Chapter Four

The thunderstorm quickly spread from the countryside to the city of Paris. Streams of water gushed along the pavements and lightning lit up the sky with bright flashes. Madame lay asleep in her gold bed. Now and again she stirred, her fingers clutching the satin coverlet. An extra loud clap of thunder woke her and she sat up, her eyes wide in horror. "Duchess! Kittens!...oh my gracious, I had the most horrible dream about them."

Climbing out of bed she lit a candle and made her way across the bedroom to the blue and gold bed close to the window where her pets always slept. "Thank goodness it was only a dream," she murmured, gently pulling back the covers.

The bed was empty! "Oh!...oh!" she stammered. "Oh, no...they're gone!"

Madame was frantic. She ran across the room and flung open the door, calling "Duchess! Kittens! Where are you?"

Her cries awoke Roquefort, the tiny mouse. "Duchess...kittens...gone? Why, that's terrible," he muttered. "Anything could happen on a night like this. They could get washed down a storm drain, struck by lightning. Oh, they'll need help. I've just got to find them," he cried.

Pulling on his red coat and matching cap, the mouse made his way to the kitty door and stepped bravely out into the rain. Rushing down the steps he called as loudly as he could, "Duchess! Kittens!" but the streets were deserted.

In their basket, Duchess and the kittens crouched together, and finally slept.

At last the light of dawn crept across the countryside. Duchess opened her eyes, and blinked once or twice. Then she remembered the awful night before and stole a glance at her sleeping kittens.

It was then she heard a voice. Yes, it was another cat...singing. Duchess looked about her. There he was, crossing the bridge, a large, powerfully-built, ginger and white tom. Duchess noticed his four snowy-white socks, his white mouth and the white ring of fur on the tip of his tail. He held it proudly, waving it in rhythm as he sang.

The singer was O'Malley, an alley cat. He crossed the bridge without a slip, then leaped into the tree directly above Duchess's head, tapping the pink blossom. A shower of petals fell onto her fur. With a smile she brushed the petals from her coat. In her social world she never, but never associated with an alley cat. This was a new experience.

The kittens crowded to the edge of the basket to peer at the stranger.

O'Malley sat down. "And what might your name be?"

"My name is Duchess."

The ginger tom was impressed. "Duchess! Beautiful! Love it! And those eyes ...oooh."

O'Malley moved closer. "Why your eyes are like sapphires sparkling so bright...they make the morning radiant and bright."

Duchess fluttered her long eyelashes. "Very poetic...but not quite Shakespeare."

O'Malley lay down. "Of course not. That's pure O'Malley, baby. Right off the cuff. Ha, ha, I got a million of 'em."

"Oh, no more please," said Duchess. "I'm really in a great deal of trouble." Her beautiful face was suddenly sad.

"Trouble?" replied O'Malley. "Helping beautiful damsels in distress is my specialty. Now, what's the hang up, your Ladyship?" The tom cat moved closer.

"Well, it is most important that I get back to Paris, so if you would just be so kind and show me the way!"

"Show you the way? Perish the thought." O'Malley stood up and leaned against Duchess, rubbing her soft fur. "We shall fly back to Paris on a magic carpet. Side by side...just the two of us."

Marie, Toulouse, and Berlioz scrambled

from the basket. O'Malley's eyes widened in surprise.

Duchess smiled. "Oh yes, M'sieu O'Malley. These are my children."

O'Malley gulped. "Oh...how sweet."

"Do you really have a magic carpet?" asked Berlioz.

"And are we really gonna ride on it?" cut in Marie.

O'Malley stalled for time, "Well...now, ah... what I meant, you see..."

"I understand you perfectly, M'sieu O'Malley," said Duchess in cool tones, then turned her back on him. "Well, come along, darlings," she called to her children. The kittens followed their mother along the river bank.

"Now that's quite a family," said O'Malley. He stroked his chin. What was he thinking of, letting those well-bred city cats go off alone to face heaven-knew-what perils. Surely he could help in some way. "Hey, hold up there," he yelled.

He approached the small group. "Now look, kids, if I said magic carpet ride, magic carpet ride it's gonna be." The three kittens stared at him. "Yeah, and it's gonna stop for passengers right here."

Duchess sat on the grass and raised her eyebrows. "Another flight into the fantasy, M'sieu O'Malley?"

"No,no, baby." O'Malley assured her. He herded the cats across the grass to the roadside. Pointing to a small clump of bushes, he said "Now, you just hide over there and you leave the rest to Thomas O'Malley."

The family took cover and O'Malley quickly climbed a tree to watch the highway. A milk truck was moving along the road towards them. "One magic carpet coming right up," he yelled.

O'Malley sprang like a mountain lion towards the truck. He landed with a thump on its hood. The milkman yelled at the sight of a huge, fierce, orange-colored cat hanging upside down and screaming, spitting and making faces at him through the windshield. The truck swerved to the edge of the road where Duchess and the kittens were hiding. The engine stalled and the truck came to a stop. Like lightning, O'Malley leaped to the road and ran for cover.

"Stupid cat! Brainless lunatic!" grumbled the milkman. He started to crank the engine.

This was the chance O'Malley had hoped for. He led Duchess and the kittens from their hiding place to the back of the truck. "All right. All aboard for Paris."The kittens jumped onto the tailgate of the truck.

"Why, Mister O'Malley, you could have lost your life." Duchess joined her family on the truck then leaned out and whispered, "How can we ever thank you?"

"My pleasure entirely," said O'Malley.

The milkman finally got the engine started, unaware that he now had passengers. He jumped into the driver's seat and pulled away from the curb.

"Bye!" called Marie waving. Then she let out a tiny scream as the truck jolted and she tumbled to the ground. "Mama!" she wailed as the milk truck moved farther and farther away.

O'Malley rushed to the rescue. Quick as a flash he grabbed Marie in his mouth and ran after the truck. Almost level with the tailgate he jumped up and gave her to her mother. Duchess had tears of joy in her eyes as she hugged her kitten.

O'Malley decided he might as well climb on board. "When we get to Paris, I'll show you the time of your life," he promised.

Duchess looked troubled. "We just

couldn't. You see, my mistress will be so worried about us."

"Humans don't worry too much about their pets," replied O'Malley.

Duchess tried to explain. "Oh, no...you don't understand. She loves us very much. Poor Madame." And she began to sing softly:

In that big mansion all alone,
In all our days, in tender ways,
Her love for us was shown;
And so you see, we can't leave her alone!
She'd always say that we're the greatest
    treasure she could own;
Because with us she never felt alone.

The kittens cuddled close to their mother and O'Malley gulped. It must be wonderful to know a human being like that - one who really cared!

Chapter Five

Roquefort, the tiny mouse, walked gloomily towards the stables at the back of the mansion. His red coat and hat were soaked, his spirits drooping. All night he had searched the streets of Paris for Duchess and her kittens, but it was no use.

Frou-Frou was waiting. "Oh, Roquefort. Did you have any luck at all?"

The mouse shook his head. "Oh. It's a sad day for all of us."

The two friends turned their heads in surprise when they heard Edgar approaching the barn door humming a happy tune. The animals looked at each other. Why was he so happy? You would think he'd be as sad as the rest of the household.

"Mornin' Frou-Frou, my pretty steed. Can you keep a secret?" he chuckled. He held a newspaper in front of Frou-Frou's eyes. "Look Frou-Frou, I've made the headlines. 'Mysterious Catnapper Abducts Family of Cats.' Aren't you proud of me?" giggled Edgar. "The police said it was a professional job. The work of a genius," Edgar bragged.

In the milk truck, traveling towards Paris, Duchess, O'Malley and the kittens were peering out over the tailgate. The kittens' tummies were feeling pretty empty.

"Anyone for breakfast?" asked O'Malley whipping the cover off a silver can with 'Cream' written on the side in large letters. The three kittens rushed forward and started lapping.

But at that moment the driver happened to look in the rearview mirror. His face turned red with anger. "Thieves! Robbers!" he yelled. Duchess, O'Malley and the kittens jumped off the truck and ran for cover. The driver hurled a wrench and a bucket after the running cats and would have hit Marie. O'Malley pulled her out of the way just in time. Together they ran across the railroad tracks and into a tool shed. Later, when the coast was clear, Duchess peered out the door. "What a horrible human!"

"Some humans are like that, Duchess," said O'Malley. "I've learned to live with them."

Duchess gave a long sigh. "I'll be so glad when we get back home."

"Well that's a long way off...so we better get movin'," replied O'Malley.

Duchess and the kittens left the shed and followed O'Malley across the railroad tracks.

"Gee whiz...look at that bridge," cried Berlioz.

"Let's play train," said Toulouse.

The kittens formed a train with Marie as caboose and set off over the bridge. "Choo,choo, choo, choo, clickety clack." The kittens were enjoying this game until there was the sharp whistle of a real

train...and it was roaring at top speed right for the kittens.

"Oh, no!" cried Duchess dashing to the tracks to protect her family.

"Down underneath here," said O'Malley pushing Duchess and the kittens on to the lower planks in the center of the tracks. Almost at once the train was on top of them. The wheels roared on either side of them as they clung together.

As soon as the danger was over Marie panicked and rolled down the hill - right into the river. "Mama!" she wailed. The water was deep and she couldn't swim.

"Oh, Marie," Duchess cried out. Her dear children were always getting into big trouble.

O'Malley dove straight into the water, calling, "Keep your head up, Marie. Here I come." He managed to catch her in his mouth and drag her towards a log. The current was strong and the log began to drift away. Quickly Duchess climbed a tree that hung out over the water.

"Thomas! Thomas! Up here," she called.

Just as the log swirled past, O'Malley was able to flip Marie into the air. Duchess made a wild grab and caught her.

But problems were by no means over for Thomas O'Malley. He had managed to climb on to the log, but he was being carried away on the strong current.

Just at this time, two white geese came struggling over the top of a hill. Named Amelia and Abigail, they were sisters on holiday from England. "What beautiful countryside," remarked Abigail.

"Yes," agreed Amelia. "So much like our own dear England." She glanced toward the river. "I say, look over there," she said in surprise. Her sister's eyes widened. O'Malley, trying to save himself, was clutching a willow branch that was overhanging the water.

"Fancy that...a cat learning to swim. He's going about it all the wrong way."

"We must correct him," said Abigail. She always insisted that everything be done in the correct manner.

The two geese waddled down the bank

and slipped into the river. "Sir..sir," cried Amelia as they swam toward a cold, wet O'Malley. "We're here to help you. You will never learn to swim properly with that willow branch in your mouth." She bit into O'Malley's lifeline. "Snip, Snip. Here we go!"

"Don't do that! Blub!" screeched O'Malley. Then he sank like a stone under the water.

"Oh, he takes to water like a fish, doesn't he?" said Abigail.

Bubbles began to form on the surface of the water. The geese looked worried.

"Gracious, Amelia...you don't suppose...?"

Amelia realized what her sister meant. Poor O'Malley might be drowning!

The two sisters dove down to the bottom of the river bed.

Chapter Six

It seemed forever before they surfaced, holding between them a very soggy cat.

"Look, Mama, there he is," cried Berlioz.

The geese brought O'Malley towards the shore. "You really did quite well for a beginner," said Abigail.

Thomas O'Malley didn't care how well he had done...he only wanted to feel firm ground beneath his paws.

"Oh, Thomas, thank goodness you're safe," purred Duchess.

"Can I help you, Mr. O'Malley? Huh?" said Toulouse.

"Help?" sputtered O'Malley. "I've had all the help I can take." Shaking himself he walked slowly onto the river bank, a sorry bedraggled sight.

Duchess and Marie introduced themselves to the geese. "Well I'm Amelia Gabble and this is my sister Abigail Gabble," said Amelia.

"Get those two web-footed lifeguards out of here," said O'Malley as he wrung out his tail.

"Now, Thomas," said Duchess. "Thomas is a dear friend of ours. He's helping us to get to Paris."

"We're going to Paris ourselves," said Amelia. "Why don't you join us?"

"I think that's a splendid idea," answered Duchess.

"Oh, no!" groaned O'Malley.

The two geese began organizing the group into a 'V' formation. "Now think goose," ordered Abigail. "Forward march!"

The two geese led the strange formation while Duchess, O'Malley and the kittens followed, trying to copy the awkward waddle of their leaders.

"Mama," asked Berlioz. "Do we have to waddle like they do?"

"Yes, dear," replied Duchess. "Think goose."

Chapter Seven

When they reached Paris, Abigail and Amelia left with their Uncle Waldo. O'Malley stroked his whiskers as he watched the three geese waddle around the corner. The district where Duchess lived was a good distance away. It was late and had been a long day for everyone. The idea occurred to O'Malley that he might take the family to his pad for the night. It was much closer.

Duchess turned her shining eyes on the cat who had been such a friend in time of need. "Thomas, Madame will be so worried. Are you sure we can't get home tonight?"

"Mama, I'm tired," complained Marie.

"Me, too!" said Berlioz. "And my feet hurt."

"I'll bet we walked a hundred miles," said Toulouse.

Duchess turned to the children. "Now, now, darlings, cheer up. Mr. O'Malley knows of a place where we can stay tonight."

"How much farther is it, Mr. O'Malley?" asked Toulouse, following O'Malley and the other cats up onto a tall roof.

O'Malley grinned. "Keep your whiskers up, Tiger. It's just beyond that next chimney pot. Well, there it is," pointed O'Malley. "My own penthouse pad. It's not exactly the Ritz, but it's peaceful and quiet and you'll..."

O'Malley was interrupted by a long blast of hot jazz music. He scratched his head. "Ahhh...oh no! Sounds like Scat Cat and his gang have dropped by."

"Oh? Friends of yours?" asked Duchess.

"Uh huh. Yeah! They're old buddies and they're...they're real swingers." O'Malley wondered what Duchess's reaction would be. "Uh...you know, not exactly your type, Duchess. Maybe we'd better find another place."

Already the kittens were scampering towards the attic window. "Oh no, no. I would like to see your pad and meet your Scat Cat," Duchess insisted.

O'Malley's pad was a bit shabby but comfortable. But it was O'Malley's guests that made Duchess start in surprise. There were cats everywhere. Cats of all sizes and colors: black, gray, orange and tortoiseshell - thin cats, fat cats, handsome cats and down-and-out alley cats. Anywhere and everywhere they sat or sprawled while they played their instruments. Scat Cat, their leader with a trumpet, was a gray cat who wore a bowler hat and a red bow-tie.

O'Malley waved. "Hey Scat Cat, blow some of that sweet stuff my way."

Scat Cat laughed. "Well lookie here...big man O'Malley is back in his alley. Swing on down here, daddy." The two cats shook hands.

One by one the members of the band called their greetings until O'Malley nudged Scat Cat forward to introduce him

to Duchess. O'Malley said proudly, "Duchess, this is the greatest cat of them all."

Smiling, Duchess held out her paw. "I'm delighted to meet you, M'sieu Scat Cat."

Scat Cat swept off his bowler and kissed her snowy paw. "Likewise, Duchess. You're too much."

Berlioz and Toulouse played the piano together while O'Malley, Scat Cat and Marie harmonized:

Everybody wants to be a cat,

Because a cat's the only cat
Who knows where it's at;
When playing jazz you always has
A welcome mat...'cause everybody
Digs a swinging cat!

"Oh boy, fellas," yelled the Chinese drummer. "Let's rock the joint!"

This was the signal for everyone to let their hair down.

Scat Cat patted Toulouse on the head and then handed him the horn. "Blow it, small fry..blow it." Toulouse grabbed the horn and blew and blew.

The other musicians climbed up on top of the piano and danced. The neighborhood was rocking with the rhythm. Perhaps it was the noise and the vibration, or maybe the dancing, but suddenly the piano tilted and then dropped right through the floor to the ground. The cats continued to sing and dance: "Everybody...everybody wants to be a cat." They danced right out of the door and onto the street. Duchess, O'Malley and the kittens watched from the attic window until they were out of sight.

The night had been exciting but now the kittens were really droopy. Duchess tucked them all in bed, making sure they were snug and cozy. "Happy dreams, my loves," she whispered.

Duchess joined Thomas O'Malley who was sitting on the window ledge staring at Paris in the moonlight. "Thomas," Duchess said, "your friends are really delightful. I just love them."

"Well, they're kind of rough around the edges, but if you're ever in a jam...wham! They're right there."

Duchess looked at O'Malley. "And wham...when we needed you, you were right there."

"Those little kittens, Duchess...I love 'em," said O'Malley.

"And they are very fond of you," said Duchess.

O'Malley moved closer and curled his tail around Duchess. They made a pretty picture sitting in the moonlight. He whispered, "Well, you know they need a..well...a father around."

Duchess rubbed her face gently against O'Malley's cheek. "Oh, Thomas, that would be wonderful. Oh, darling, if only I could."

"But, why can't you?" asked O'Malley.

Duchess's shoulders sagged. "Because of Madame...I could never leave her."

"But Madame is a human. You're just one of her house pets," said O'Malley.

"Oh, no!" insisted Duchess. "We mean far more to her than that. Oh, I'm sorry but we just have to go home tomorrow."

O'Malley shrugged, trying to hide his disappointment. "Well, I guess you know best. But I'm gonna miss you, baby. And I'm gonna miss the kids, too. Goodnight, Duchess."

"Goodnight, Thomas," whispered Duchess, a big lump in her throat.

Chapter Eight

The next morning dawned warm and sunny. Duchess felt sad at heart. She and Thomas O'Malley were soon to part. Thomas had provided a good breakfast for the family and now they were heading along streets leading towards Madame's home. For the sake of the kittens, Duchess put on a cheerful face.

"Hey, meow!" O'Malley whistled. "What a classy neighborhood. Dig those fancy wigwams."

"Let's hurry," said Duchess. "We're almost home."

Roquefort was perched on a window ledge gazing up the street. Suddenly his face lit up. "Duchess! Kittens! They're back!" he cried. He slid down the curtain and dashed into the next room. He pulled up short. Edgar was sitting drinking wine. "Oh, no. Edgar! I've got to do something quick." What could he do to protect Duchess and the kittens from this greedy man?

Edgar leaned forward to take another bottle of champagne from the ice bucket. "Edgar, old chap, get used to the finer things in life," he said to himself. "Someday they're all going to be yours, you sly fox."

Roquefort, because he couldn't think of anything else to do, crept up and tied the butler's shoelaces together.

Meanwhile the kittens had squeezed through the railings around the mansion. "Hurray! We're home!" yelled Toulouse.

Marie chased after her brother. "Wait for me!" she called. Together they bounded up the steps to their kitty door. They jumped at the door but to their surprise, it was locked.

"Come on. Let's start meowing," said Marie. The kittens took her advice and all started meowing as loudly as they could. The sound reached Edgar's ears. His face turned red with anger as he spat out a mouthful of wine.

"It can't be them," he muttered, torn between anger and fear.

Edgar leapt to his feet, but because his shoelaces were tied together he stumbled and fell. Roquefort ran for the kitty door and yelled, "Don't come in! Go away!"

But the kittens were making such a racket that they didn't hear him.

Duchess and O'Malley were standing together at the gate. They both looked unhappy. "Maybe just a short, sweet goodbye would be easiest," said O'Malley.

"I'll never forget you, Thomas O'Malley," promised Duchess.

"So long, baby," said O'Malley as he turned away from the gates of the mansion.

Duchess joined her kittens on the porch. She didn't hear Roquefort shout, "Don't come in. Look out for Edgar!" But it was too late. The kitty door opened and the family went in.

Edgar waited as they trooped in. His narrow eyes were gleaming. He had a large sack hidden behind his back. "Duchess, wherever have you been?" he asked.

"Look out for the sack!" yelled the mouse. The warning came too late for the sack came down on Duchess and her three kittens. Once again they were prisoners of the wicked butler.

Edgar was tying a knot in the top of the sack when he heard footsteps. Madame called, "Edgar! Edgar! Come quickly!" Edgar flung the sack into the unlit oven. "I'll take care of you later," he growled.

"They're back! I heard them!" said Madame. "Quickly open the door and let them in." Edgar opened the main door and Madame rushed out calling, "Duchess! Kittens! Come here, my darlings!"

In the kitchen, Roquefort had climbed on to the handle of the oven and was talking to Duchess. "His name is O'what?" asked the mouse.

Duchess's voice was muffled. "His name is O'Malley," she repeated. "O'Malley! Just run. Go get him!"

"Yes, yes. I'm on my way!" said Roquefort as he landed with a thump on the floor.

On the porch Madame wrung her hands. Suddenly she looked very pale and tired. "Oh, it's no use, Edgar. It was just the imagination of an old lady. But I thought I heard them."

"I'm so sorry, Madame," smirked Edgar.

Roquefort dashed through the mansion gates and looked up and down the street for O'Malley. He was nowhere in sight. The mouse didn't have time to think, so he turned right and hoped he was correct. He turned a corner and presto! There was O'Malley.

"Mr. O'Malley," he called. "Hey! Stop!"

The cat turned. A mouse chasing him? This was a switch. Before he had time to speak the mouse flung himself between the cat's claws. "Duchess ... kittens ... in

trouble...butler did it," the mouse said breathlessly.

"Duchess and the kittens in trouble? Go get Scat Cat and his gang of alley cats.."

"Alley cats?" said Roquefort, his voice shaking. "But I'm a mouse."

"Look, I'm gonna need help," snapped O'Malley.

"You mean you want me to..." Roquefort trembled.

"Move!" ordered O'Malley. "Just tell 'em O'Malley sent you...and you won't have a bit of trouble."

Roquefort was not convinced. Apart from Duchess and her family, all cats spelled trouble.

Despite his fears, the brave little mouse tracked down Scat Cat and his gang. "Oh please...ah, I was sent here for help...by a cat," squeaked Roquefort. "O'Malley needs help. Duchess and the kittens are in trouble."

Scat Cat sprang into action. "Come on, cats, we gotta split," said the leader. They tore off up the street, the tiny white and gray mouse chasing them.

"Hey! Wait for me!" screeched Roquefort. "You don't know the way!"

A Frenchman was at a table outside, drinking wine. He blinked, stared, then rubbed his eyes. A mouse chasing a gang of cats? He shook his head as he poured the rest of the wine into the gutter.

Chapter Nine

When Roquefort left to find Scat Cat, O'Malley rushed at whirlwind speed up the driveway leading to the mansion. Leaping onto a window ledge, he was in time to see the wicked butler speaking on the phone. Edgar hung up, an evil smile on his face. Leaning forward he grabbed a bulky sack lying at his feet and hurried towards the barn. O'Malley followed.

"Now my little pesky pets, you're going to travel first class in your own private compartment," said Edgar. He put the sack containing Duchess and the kittens into a large trunk. On the outside of the trunk there was a printed label that said,"To Timbuktu, Equatorial Africa."

Edgar chuckled as he closed the lid, then

locked it. "All the way to Timbuktu. And this time...you'll never come back."

O'Malley's eyes flashed in anger. Silent as a shadow, he jumped to the loft, and prepared to pounce. Edgar pushed the trunk across the floor toward Frou-Frou.

The mare watched in horror. Edgar breathed in little gasps. The trunk was heavy. "Oh...we...we have to hurry. The baggage truck will be here any moment."

"So," said O'Malley to himself, "that was who the butler was talking to on the phone." He drew back and with his ears pressed close to his head he sprang through the air with a wild, blood-curdling screech. Edgar was so surprised he fell across the trunk as O'Malley landed in the center of his back, claws outstretched.

"Ohhhh..." screamed Edgar in terror, trying to throw off the furry fury. He ran towards Frou-Frou. She grabbed the butler's coat tails. A tug of war began as Edgar pushed the trunk towards the door and Frou-Frou pulled him back.

O'Malley ran into the open but Edgar took aim and hurled a pitchfork at the cat. Frou-Frou whinnied in fright, sure that this time O'Malley was done for. Luckily it missed spearing the tom cat, but it did imprison him between the prongs.

Grinning, Edgar turned to make his escape, but too late. As he reached the barn door, Scat Cat and his gang arrived. Edgar and the cats fought a furious battle. Snarling, spitting, clawing and yowling, the gang showed no mercy.

Meanwhile Roquefort hurried to the trunk and began working on the lock. O'Malley managed to free himself from the pitchfork and ran to the trunk to help Roquefort lift the lid.

"You're going to Timbuktu if it's the last thing I do," promised Edgar. The snarling band of cats leaped on him but he climbed on top of the trunk, grabbed a club and began swinging at them.

The Russian cat sprang into action. Untying a rope from a pulley, he loosened a bale of hay that fell on Edgar's head.

The Chinese cat flung down a horse collar that pinned the butler's arms to his sides. Scat Cat half drowned him with a bucket of water. Edgar struggled...but now he was on the losing side of the battle.

Now they hooked a fishing line on Frou-Frou's horse collar and she pulled Edgar off the top of the trunk. The gang lost no time raising the lid. Duchess and her kittens were free! Now it was the butler's turn to be dropped inside the trunk and the lid closed. Everyone pushed and the trunk bumped and slid out of the barn and into the yard.

Seconds later, a truck backed into the courtyard and two men jumped out. If they had looked toward the barn they would have seen a gang of cats, a horse and a mouse all peeking from the dusty window.

"Well, Mac," said the driver scratching his head. "This must be the trunk going to Timbuktu."

The men heaved the trunk into the truck and drove away. The animals crowded at the window all cheered.

Chapter Ten

That evening Madame was taking a family photograph. Her family...her very dear family had been restored to her and her heart was full.

Duchess, O'Malley and the three kittens were posed on the blue velvet sofa. "Good! Good!" said Madame looking out from the hood over the camera. "Duchess," she said, "It's wonderful to have you all back...and I think this young man is very handsome. Shall we keep him in the family?"

"Meow! Meow! Meow!" answered the three kittens.

Madame nodded and returned to the camera. "Of course we will. We need a man around the house."

Duchess looked shyly at O'Malley and his heart beat fast as he looked into her sapphire blue eyes. "Now don't move," said Madame. "Smile. Say cheese."

Roquefort came out of his hole. "Did someone say cheese?"